# One-o-saur, Two-o-saur

## David Bedford and Leonie Worthington

LITTLE HARE

1

One-o-saur hopping on one Leg.

**2**

Two-o-saurs hatching from eggs.

Three-o-saurs swinging on swings.

# 4 Four-o-saurs on a Trampoline.

5

Five-o-saurs wearing fancy hats.

Six-o-saurs cuddling cats.

7

Seven-o-saurs banging on drums.

Eight-o-saurs missing Their mums.

# Nine-o-saurs waiting To be fed.

10

Ten-o-saurs standing on their heads.

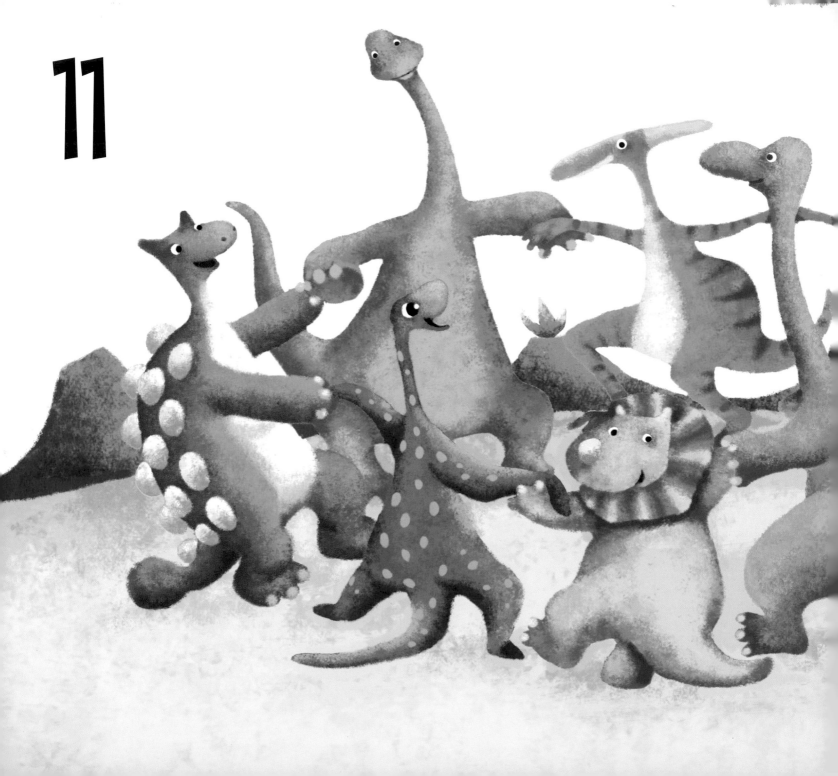

11

Eleven-o-saurs all in a spin.

Twelve-o-saurs jumping in.

*For Isobel-o-saur—DB*
*For Hugh, Jack and Phoebe—LW*

Little Hare Books
4/21 Mary Street, Surry Hills
NSW 2010 AUSTRALIA

www.littleharebooks.com

Copyright © text David Bedford 2005
Copyright © illustrations Leonie Worthington 2005

*First published in 2005*

National Library of Australia
Cataloguing-in-Publication entry

Bedford, David, 1969-.
*One-o-saur, two-o-saur.*

For pre-school children.
ISBN 1 877003 84 0.

1. Counting – Juvenile literature. 2. Dinosaurs – Juvenile
literature. I. Worthington, Leonie, 1956-. II. Title.

513.211

Designed by Serious Business
Produced by Phoenix Offset, Hong Kong
Printed in China

5 4 3 2 1